Gwangju, Cross of Our Nation

아아 광주여, 우리나라의 십자가여

Gwangju, Cross of Our Nation

poems, 2014 / KIM JUN TAE

Printed in the Republic of Korea.
Published in Seoul, by Hansmedia.
Address: 121-838, (Seogyo-dong, Kangwon Building 5F) 13,
Yanghwa-ro-11-gil, Mapo-gu, Seoul, Korea.
Tel: 82-2-707-0337
Fax: 82-2-707-0198
Web site: www.hansmedia.com

FIRST EDITION

ISBN: 978-89-5975-783-1 03810

Gwangju, Cross of Our Nation

아아 광주여, 우리나라의 십자가여

poems by Kim Jun Tae

김준태 영역시집

Translated by

David R. Macann
Chae-Pyong Song & Melanie Steyn
Chun Kyung Ja
Kevin Ilsub Lim

HANSMEDIA 한스미디어

devoted to 'May Spirits', the Life as Sky_Earth,
the people who fought for the oneness of World

이 시집을 오월영령과 하늘땅 같은 사람의 생명,
하나됨의 세상을 위해 싸운 사람들에게 바친다.

CONTENTS

차례

Since the example of South Korea's speedy modernization is so rare in world, as rare is it's permeation of most complicated tragedy. Kim Jun Tae, he is one of the few poets whom the history of modern Korea's ordeals themselves, by need of their own, called. Without his poems, there was not a most important vessel to contain them as a whole.

His early, the rare and stout rural modernist aesthetic, meeting the 'Gwanju Cruelty', with Christian blaze, seemed to explode but exploded not. Meeting the dearest wish of South-North unification, with Mother-Earth's love, seemed to explode but exploded not. On the contrary, achieves the more deep broad mind's 'mold of tears'.

He is now one of the greatest grandpa poets, and reading his 'late-masterpiece' poems are enough to make us realize how much we are, beyond fortunate, blessed as humans unhappy having known unhappiness have a capacity to weep, to pity. Now with his poems, the Korea's sad modern history wins a meanings of sadness that are possible only to humans.

Kim Jung Whan, Poet

한국만큼 빠른 근대화를 이룬 사례가 세계에 드물기에, 한국의 근대화만큼 복잡한 비극으로 침윤된 사례도 없다. 김준태, 그는 수난의 한국현대사 그 자체가 자신의 필요로 불러낸 몇 안 되는 시인이다. 그의 시가 없었다면 그것을 통째 담아낼 매우 중요한 시의 그릇이 없었다.

초기의, 그 희귀하고 강건한 농촌-모더니즘 미학이 '광주' 참혹을 만나 기독교적 화염으로, 폭발하는 것 같았으나 폭발하지 않았다. 남북통일 염원을 만나 대지적인 사랑으로, 폭발하는 것 같았으나 폭발하지 않았다. 오히려, 깊어진 너그러움이 눈물의 거푸집에 달했다.

그는 지금 가장 위대한 할아버지 시인 중 하나이고, '만년의 걸작'에 달한 그의 작품을 읽으면, 불행을 알기에 불행한 인간이 눈물을 흘릴 수 있다는 게 다행을 넘어, 얼마나 축복인가를 깨닫게 해주기에 족하다. 지금 그의 시가 있으므로, 슬픈 현대사가 비로소, 인간 말고는 알 수 없는 슬픔의 의미에 달한다.

시인 김정환

A bird

flies in the sky,

Take a look!

Man

flies even out of the sky.

Lately my topic for poetry writing has become 'about man' more and more. I'd like to give all the right for life to the men and I am sinking into the desperate craving to create the most beautiful song that I can sing. Like the poem I mentioned above, man believes that he can fly in and even out of the sky with pleasure and sorrow.

Man and life, how wonderful and endless they are! I used to say "Nothing in This World Vanishes." while Friedrich von Schiller lamented "Even all the beautiful things have gone(Auch das Schöne muß sterben)." I have clearly observed the people who "drive away death with death and seek life with death[Gwangju, Cross of Our Nation]" with my own eyes and once I was possessed by such a spirit.

As Goethe said, poets should see the big picture like the eagles which do not realize they are crossing the border. A big thanks to all who participated in translating in English, Chinese and Japanese: Professor David R. Macann from Harvard University, Professor Rick Chu(Joo Lib Hee) from Taipei, editors for the Japanese magazine "The World(世界)". Professor Chae-pyong Song from Maryglove College in the U.S.A., Chun Kyung Ja working for UNESCO, and Kevin Ilsub Lim in New York.

I want to express my special appreciation for Oh Jae Yiel, Chairperson of The May 18 Memorial Foundation and Suh Chae Hong, president of Chosun University, the poet Kim Jung Hwan and Kim Gi Ok, the president of Hansmedia, for kindly publishing this edition. I devote my poems and songs to all the people visiting the dreaming city Gwangju and Korea like giving flowers in their hair.

Dec. 2014

Kim Jun Tae

새는

하늘을 날고

봐—

사람은

하늘 밖까지 날은다.

   요즘 들어서 나의 시의 화두는 더욱 '사람'에게 모아지는 것 같다. 사람에게 이 세상 생명체의 모든 권위를 부여하면서 내가 부를 수 있는 아름다운 노래의 절정을 보여주고 싶다는 열망에 깊숙이 젖는다. 적어도 사람은 '하늘'만이 아니라 '하늘 밖'까지 날아다닌다고 믿고 또한 슬퍼하면서 즐거워한다.

   사람과 사람생명, 아 얼마나 아름답고 영원한 것인가! 프리드리히 쉴러는 "아름다운 것조차 사라져버린다(Auch das Schöne muß sterben)"고 한탄했지만 그러나 나는 "이 세상에서 사라지는 것은 하나도 없다(Nothing in This World Vanishes)"고 노래한 적이 있다. "죽음으로써 죽음을 물리치고 죽음으로써 삶을 찾으려했던(has tried to drive away death with death, and to seek life with death) [아아 광주여, 우리나라의 십자가여]" 사람들을 일찍이 나는 두 눈으로 똑똑히 보았으며 엑스타시 상태에 들기도 했다.

모름지기 시인은 자기 나라의 국경을 넘으면서도 국경을 넘은지도 모르는 독수리처럼 그렇게 눈이 커야 한다는 괴테의 말이 생각난다. 영어와 중국어, 일본어 등의 번역에 참여해주신 하버드 대학 데이비드 R. 맥캔 교수, 타이베이의 주립회 교수, 일본의 『산케이(世界)』 잡지 편집인, 시카고 메리글로브 대학 송재평 교수, 유네스코에서 일하시는 천경자 선생, 뉴욕에서 일하시는 캐빈 일섭 임 선생께 두루 감사드린다.

시집이 나오는 데 우정을 베풀어주신 오재일 5·18기념재단 이사장과 서재홍 조선대학교 총장, 그리고 김정환 시인과 한스미디어 김기옥 사장께 감사드린다. 마치 머리에 꽃을 꽂아주듯이 코리아와 늘 꿈꾸는 도시 광주를 찾아오시는 모든 사람들에게 여기, 시와 노래를 바친다.

2014년 12월
김준태

Part 1

Gwangju, Cross of Our Nation

啊啊, 光州唷! 我們國家的十字架唷!

ああ, 光州よ, わが国の十字架よ

Oh, Gwangju! The Cross of Our Nation!

아아 광주여, 우리나라의 십자가여

제1부

Gwangju, Cross of Our Nation

啊啊, 光州唷! 我們國家的十字架唷!

ああ, 光州よ, わが国の十字架よ

Oh, Gwangju! The Cross of Our Nation!

아아 광주여, 우리나라의 십자가여

Gwangju, Cross of Our Nation

O Gwangju, and Mudung Mountain.

Between death and more death,

City of our eternal youth, flowing

with blood and tears!

Our father: Where has he gone?

Mother: Where has she fallen?

Our sons:

Where were they killed and buried?

And our lovely daughters:

Where are they lying, mouths agape?

Where were our spirits

torn apart, ripped to shreds?

Gwangju, by the flocks of birds

and by God as well

abandoned: City of our bloody wounds,

where the truly human

beings still abide, dawn to dark

thrown down, beaten, and yet rising again.

In death refusing

and through death seeking life.

Province of Lamentation! Phoenix!

Though the sea winds tumble down headlong,

and all the other mountains of this age

tower up in a sham,

no one can rip,

no one can steal

this banner, Freedom's,

banner of humanity,

with flesh and bone given life

at the core.

City of our!

our songs, our dreams, our love

at times mount up like great waves,

at times like an ancient tomb

collapse, and yet

Gwangju! O, Gwangju!

Shouldering the cross of this nation,

He climbs over Mudung Mountain,

over Golgotha, the Son of Heaven,

on his body

the wounds,

the death.

Truly we have died.

We who cannot love this land,

who cannot love our children

have died.

Truly we have died.

From Chung-jang Road, and Kum-nam;

From Hwa-chong Block, from San-su and Yongbong,

Chi-san, Yang-dong, Kye-rim,

and on, and on......

O wind that has blown down upon us, swallowing

our blood and pieces of flesh!

Ceaseless futility of life!

Thrown down again and again,

in weeping all that is left us?

To draw a breath: is that all

of terror and of life?

Those who have survived

hang their heads in guilt.

Those who have survived

have all lost their souls.

To face a bowl of rice

is too difficult, too frightening

to do.

"I died, my love, waiting

for you, waiting outside the gate

for you ......

Why was it my life they robbed?

It was our lot to live

in a rented room, but how much gladness we knew!

How I wanted to proved well for you!

O, my love!

And I, with this body bearing life

have now found death. My love,

forgive me. My love,

your child, yours ......

O, my love, I have ended

by killing you."

O Gwangju! Mudung Mountain!

piercing the very center of death

and emerging, city

of our eternal youth, vibrant

with the fluttering white cotton sleeves!

Phoenix

   that you are

         Phoenix!

         Phoenix!

Bearing the cross of this land

returning over Golgotha,

Son of our nation's god:

Jesus who once died

and rose again:

Has he not lived until today,

and forever?

And we who have died by the hundreds,

our true love will return to life.

Our fire! Our glory! Our pain!

Even more surely, we shall survive.

Our strength increases, and even we

shall rise into the blue heavens

and touch our lips to the sun and moon.

O Gwangju! O Mudung Mountain!

Our eternal banner,

dream,

and cross.

Even as life flows on,

City of Youth

may you be ever younger.

For now we are sure,

gathering together. Hands joined

in sure affirmation,

We have risen.

* 「Gwangju, Cross of Our Nation」 was translated by David R. Macann. He is a professor of English literature at Harvard University. This poem, published on June 2, 1980 in The Chonnam Daily is a truth and manifesto about Gwangju Uprising. With the publication of this poem, the newspaper was forced to shut down, and the poet was laid off from his teaching at Chonnam High School. This poem has been acclaimed as the first poem that addressed the uprising.

啊啊，光州唷！我們國家的十字架唷！

啊啊，光州唷 無等山唷

在死亡與死亡之間

血淚汩汩而流

我們永遠的青春之都唷

我們的父親哪裡去了

我們的母親倒在哪裡

我們的孩子

死在哪裡 埋在哪裡

我們可愛的女兒 又在哪裡 張著嘴 橫陳著

我們的靈魂 又在哪裡

被撕成零碎破片而丟棄

連上帝 連鳥群

都遺棄的光州唷

但有血性的人

仍朝暮活著

跌倒 摔倒 再站起來

沾滿我們鮮血的都市唷

以死亡來對抗死亡

以死亡來尋求生命的

啊啊 只有慟哭的南道的

不死鳥 不死鳥 不死鳥唷

日月顛倒

這時代所有的山巒

輪廓聳起之際

但誰也不能撕裂

不能搶奪

啊,自由的旗幟唷

用肉與骨編織的旗幟唷

啊 我們的都市

我們的歌謠與夢想與愛情

有時被波濤推移

有時被墳墓掩埋

啊,光州 光州唷

背負這個國家的十字架

越過無等山

越過谷高多山坡

啊,全身只有傷痕

只有死亡 老天之子唷

我們真的死了嗎

不能再愛這個國家

不能再愛我們的孩子們地死了嗎

我們真的永遠死了嗎

在忠壯路 在錦南路

在華亭洞 在山水洞 在龍鳳洞

在池院洞 在良洞 在雞林洞

還有 還有 還有 ……

啊, 颱來的風吞噬了

我們的血與肉塊

無奈的歲月流逝

啊 活著的人

全都像罪犯一樣低垂著頭

活著的人全都

失魂了 連面對飯碗

都很難 很害怕

不害怕都不行

（親愛的 我在等你

走出門外去等你

我死了

為什麼要奪走我的生命

不 奪走你的全部

我們租屋過日子

但我們是多麼幸福

我想要把你照顧好

啊 親愛的

我是懷著身孕的身軀

那樣地死去 親愛的！

對不起 親愛的！

我的生命被奪走

我是你的全部

你的青春 你的愛情

你的孩子 你的

啊啊 親愛的！ 是我殺了你嗎？）

啊 光州唷 無等山唷

衝出死亡與死亡

白衣的衣角迎風搖曳

我們永遠的青春之都唷

不死鳥 不死鳥 不死鳥 不死鳥

背負我們國家的十字架

再次越過谷高多山坡

這個國家的老天之子

耶穌死過一次

也復活一次

不止到今天 還永遠活著

但是我們死了幾百遍

也活了幾百遍的我們的摯愛

我們的光芒 榮耀悲痛

我們現在更要活下去

我們現在更堅實

我們現在更

啊 我們現在

肩併肩 骨併骨

攀上這個國家的無等山

啊 攀爬到藍天上

親吻太陽與月亮

光州 無等山唷

啊 我們永遠的旗幟

夢想 十字架唷

歲月流逝而

越年輕的青春之都

我們現在確實堅定團結

確實堅定牽手站起來

.

*主按： 最近在鑽研光州抗爭與歷史清算的過程中, 也涉獵到一些光州相關的文學藝術
創作。這首金準泰的詩, 是光州抗爭事件之後最先發表的一首, 刊登在1980年六月二日的
「全南每日新聞」第一版（兩個月後該報被軍事獨裁政權強制停刊）, 也立即被美, 日, 德
, 法等國的媒體與雜誌翻譯轉載。這首詩對後來相關的詩作有極大的啟迪與影響, 因此被
選入「光州民主化抗爭詩選」的第一篇。版主特別翻譯出來並附上韓文原作與英譯, 供大
家參考。

*詩人 金準泰, 1948年生, 畢業於光州朝鮮大學。原本擔任高中教師, 因為此詩被解聘, 後
來創作不斷, 包括抗議詩, 敘事詩, 統一詩, 以及描繪鄉村生活與感情的詩等。他一共出版
十二本詩集, 現在朝鮮大學擔任韓國文學講座, 並為「韓國文學和平論壇」副會長。

あ, 光州よ, わが国の十字架よ

金準泰 (キムジュンテ)

ああ光州 (クワンジュ) よ, 無等山 (ムトンサン) よ

死と死の間に

血の涙のみを流す

われらの永遠なる青春の都市よ

われらの父はどこに行ったか

われらの母はどこで倒れたか

われらの息子らは

どこで死に, どこに埋められたか

われらのいとおしい娘は

またどこで口をあけたまま横たわっているか

われらの魂魄はまたどこで散り散りに, こなごなになってしまったのか

神も鳥の群も

去ってしまった光州よ

しかし人間らしき人間のみが

朝夕生き残って

倒れて, 倒れてまた起ちあがる

われらの血みどろの都市よ

死で追い払い

死で生を求めようとした

ああ, 慟哭のみの南道の

不死鳥よ, 不死鳥よ, 不死鳥よ

太陽も風も逆立って

この時代のすべての山脈が

空しく聳え立っているとき

しかしその誰も引き裂くことのできない奪うことのできない

ああ, 自由の旗よ

人間の旗よ

肉と骨で固まった旗よ

ああ, われらの都市

われらの歌と夢と愛が

時には波濤のように押され

時には墓のように埋められても

ああ光州よ, 光州よ

この国の十字架を背負って

無等山を越えて

ゴルゴダの丘を越えて行く

ああ, 全身傷だらけの

死のみである神の子よ

ほんとうにわれらは死んでしまった

これ以上この国を愛することができずに

これ以上われらの子どもたちを愛することができずに死んでしまったのか

ほんとうにわれらはすっかり死んでしまったのか

忠壮路(チュンジャンロ)で, 錦南路(クムナムロ)で

花亭洞(クワジョンドン)で, 山水洞(サンスイドン)で, 龍峯洞(ヨンボンドン)で

池山洞(ジサンドン)で, 陽洞(ヤンドン)で, 鶏林洞(ケイムドン)で

そして, また, そして......

ああ, われらの血と肉を

のみくだして吹いてくる風よ

無情に流れる歳月よ

いま, われらはただ

倒れて倒れて泣かねばならないか

恐怖と生命 (いのち), どんなに

息をしなければならないのか

ああ, 生き残った人々は

みんな罪人のように頭 (こうべ) を垂れている

生き残った人々は

みんなが

気を失って, 飯の椀にさえ

向きあって坐れない, 恐しい

恐しくてどうにもできない

（あなた, あなたを待っていたのに

門の外であなたを待っていたのに

私は死にました……

どうして私の生命が奪われたのでしょう

借間生活ではあっても

どんなに私たちは幸せだったことでしょう

あたしはあなたによくしてあげたかった

ああ, あなた!

それなのに私は子どもをみごもった身体で

このように, 死んだ, あなた

すみません! あなた

あなたの子, あなたの

ああ, あなた, 私がついに

あなたの子を殺したのでしょうか）

ああ, 光州よ, 無等山よ

死と死をつきぬいて

白衣の衣 (ころも) はためく

われらの永遠なる青春の都市よ

不死鳥よ, 不死鳥よ, 不死鳥よ

この国の十字架を背負って

ゴルゴダの丘を再び越えてくる

この国の神の子よ

イエスは一たび死んで

一たびよみがえって

今日まで, いやいつまでも生きられるとか

しかしわれらは**数**百回死んでも

数百回をよみがえるわれらの真の愛よ

われらの火よ, 栄光よ, 痛みよ

いま, われらはいっそう生き**残**れる

いま, われらはいっそう強い

いま, われらはいっそう

青い空に登って

太陽と月に口づけする

光州よ，無等山よ

ああ，われらの永遠なる旗よ

夢よ，十字架よ

歳月が流れれば流れるほど

いっそう若くなれる青春の都市よ

いまわれらは確かに

固く団結している，確かに固く手を握って起ちあがる

＊参照：「世界」（416号）岩波書店，1980年 7月

Oh, Gwangju! The Cross of Our Nation!

Oh, Gwangju! Mudeung Mountain!

Our city of eternal youth

that sheds blood tears

between deaths!

Where has our father gone?

Where has our mother collapsed?

Where has our Son died and been buried?

And, where does our Daughter lie dead, her mouth gaping?

Where have our soul and spirit

gone, torn and broken into pieces?

Gwangju, which both God and birds have left!

Our blood-covered city

where decent people

are still alive, morning and evening,

collapsing, falling down, and rising again!

Ah, the phoenix, the phoenix, the phoenix

of the South Province full of wailing

that has tried to drive away death with death,

and to seek life with death!

When the sun and the moon nosedive

and all the mountain ridges

stand shamelessly high,

ah, the flag of liberty

that nobody can tear down

or take away!

The flag of humanity!

The flag, hardened with flesh and bones!

Oh, our city

where at times our songs, dreams, and love

roll like waves,

and at other times we are hidden in graves.

Oh, Gwangju, Gwangju

who carries the cross of this nation,

climbing over Mudeung Mountain,

and walks over the hill of Golgotha!

Oh, the son of God,

whose whole body is covered with wounds,

and who is the emblem of death!

Are we really quite dead?

Dead,

unable to love this country any more,

unable to love our children any more?

Are we absolutely dead?

On Chungjangro, on Kumnamro,

At Hwajungdong, at Sansoodong, at Yongbongdong

At Jisandong, at Yangdong, at Kyerimdong,

And, and, and......

Ah, the wind that blows over,

gobbling up our blood and flesh!

The hopeless flow of time!

Should we now

just collapse, fall, and cry?

Terrified of life, how should we

breathe a breath?

Oh, all those survive

lower their heads like sinners.

All those still alive have lost

spirit, and they find it difficult

even to face their rice bowls.

Afraid, they don't know what to do.

(Dear, I was killed

while I was waiting for you,

waiting for you outside the door.

Why did they take away my life?

Though we lived in a rented room,

we were quite happy.

I wanted to live, loving you.

Oh, my dear!

But I was killed like this,

pregnant with a child of yours.

I am sorry, my dear!

They took away my life from me,

and I took away everything of yours,

your youth, your love,

your son, and all.

Oh, my dear! In the end,

did I kill you?)

Oh, Gwangju! Mudeung Mountain!

Our city of eternal youth

who breaks through deaths

and flutters the ends of white clothes!

The phoenix, the phoenix, the phoenix!

The son of God of this nation

who climbs up the hill of Golgotha again,

carrying the cross of this nation!

Jesus is said to have died once

and been resurrected,

and to live till this day or rather forever.

But our true love

that would die hundreds of deaths

and yet resurrects itself hundreds of times!

Our light, glory, and pain.

Now we will be revived ever more.

Now we become ever stronger.

Now we – ever more.

Oh, now we,

putting our shoulders to shoulders, bones to bones,

climb the Mudeung Mountain of this nation.

Oh, we rise up to the oddly blue sky

to kiss the sun and the moon.

Gwangju! Mudeung Mountain!

Oh, our eternal flag!

Our dream, our cross!

The city of youth that will get younger

as time goes by!

Now we are firmly united,

surely and surely,

we hold each other's hands tight

and rise up.

* 「Oh, Gwangju! The Cross of Our Nation!」was translated by Chae-Pyong Song and Melanie
Steyn. Mr. Song(1960~2013) was a professor of English literature at Marygrove College, and
Melanie Steyn was his fellow.

아아 광주여, 우리나라의 십자가여

아아, 광주여 무등산이여
죽음과 죽음 사이에
피눈물을 흘리는
우리들의 영원한 청춘의 도시여

우리들의 아버지는 어디로 갔나
우리들의 어머니는 어디서 쓰러졌나
우리들의 아들은
어디에서 죽어 어디에 파묻혔나
우리들의 귀여운 딸은
또 어디에서 입을 벌린 채 누워 있나
우리들의 혼백은 또 어디에서
찢어져 산산이 조각나 버렸나

하느님도 새떼들도
떠나가버린 광주여
그러나 사람다운 사람들만이
아침저녁으로 살아남아
쓰러지고, 엎어지고, 다시 일어서는
우리들의 피투성이 도시여
죽음으로써 죽음을 물리치고

죽음으로써 삶을 찾으려 했던
아아 통곡뿐인 남도의
불사조여 불사조여 不死鳥여

해와 달이 곤두박질치고
이 시대의 모든 산맥들이
엉터리로 우뚝 솟아있을 때
그러나 그 누구도 찢을 수 없고
빼앗을 수 없는
아아, 자유의 깃발이여
살과 뼈로 응어리진 깃발이여

아아, 우리들의 도시
우리들의 노래와 꿈과 사랑이
때로는 파도처럼 밀리고
때로는 무덤을 뒤집어쓸지언정
아아, 광주여 광주여
이 나라의 십자가를 짊어지고
무등산을 넘어
골고다 언덕을 넘어가는

아아, 온몸에 상처뿐인
죽음뿐인 하느님의 아들이여

정말 우리는 죽어버렸나
더 이상 이 나라를 사랑할 수 없이
더 이상 우리들의 아이들을
사랑할 수 없이 죽어버렸나
정말 우리들은 아주 죽어버렸나

충장로에서 금남로에서
화정동에서 산수동에서 용봉동에서
지원동에서 양동에서 계림동에서
그리고 그리고 그리고……
아아, 우리들의 피와 살덩이를
삼키고 불어오는 바람이여
속절 없는 세월의 흐름이여

아아, 살아남은 사람들은
모두가 죄인처럼 고개를 숙이고 있구나
살아남은 사람들은 모두가
넋을 잃고 밥그릇조차 대하기

어렵구나 무섭구나

무서워 어쩌지도 못하는구나

(여보, 당신을 기다리다가

문밖에 나가 당신을 기다리다가

나는 죽었어요......그들은

왜 나의 목숨을 빼앗아갔을까요

아니 당신의 전부를 빼앗아갔을까요

셋방살이 신세였지만

얼마나 우린 행복했어요

난 당신에게 잘 해주고 싶었어요

아아, 여보!

그런데 난 아이를 밴 몸으로

이렇게 죽은 거예요 여보!

미안해요, 여보!

나에게서 나의 목숨을 빼앗아가고

나는 또 당신의 전부를

당신의 젊음 당신의 사랑

당신의 아들 당신의

아아, 여보! 내가 결국

당신을 죽인 것인가요?)

아아, 광주여 무등산이여

죽음과 죽음을 뚫고 나가

백의의 옷자락을 펄럭이는

우리들의 영원한 청춘의 도시여

불사조여 불사조여 불사조여

이 나라의 십자가를 짊어지고

골고다 언덕을 다시 넘어오는

이 나라의 하느님 아들이여

예수는 한번 죽고

한번 부활하여

오늘까지 아니 언제까지 산다던가

그러나 우리들은 몇 백 번을 죽고도

몇 백 번을 부활할 우리들의 참사랑이여

우리들의 빛이여, 영광이여, 아픔이여

지금 우리들은 더욱 살아나는구나

지금 우리들은 더욱 튼튼하구나

지금 우리들은 더욱

아아, 지금 우리들은

어깨와 어깨 뼈와 뼈를 맞대고

이 나라의 무등산을 오르는구나

아아, 미치도록 푸르른 하늘을 올라

해와 달을 입맞추는구나

광주여 무등산이여

아아, 우리들의 영원한 깃발이여

꿈이여 십자가여

세월이 흐르면 흐를수록

더욱 젊어져 갈 청춘의 도시여

지금 우리들은 확실히

굳게 뭉쳐 있다 확실히

굳게 손잡고 일어선다.

---

* 「아아 광주여, 우리나라의 십자가여」는 1980년 5월, 한반도의 남녘 도시 광주에서 공수계엄군의
총칼에 맞서 일어난 '5·18광주항쟁(Gwangju Upring)'을 최초로 형상화한 시로 동년 6월 2일자
전남매일(2개월 후 강제 폐간됨) 신문에 게재되었고 곧바로 외신을 타고 미국, 일본, 중국, 독일,
프랑스 등 전 세계 언론에 발표되었다.

Part 2

A Single Bean

Woman's Love Outruns a Bullet

Flames or Flowers?

You

Field Woman

Nothing in This World Vanishes

* Six poems of Kim Jun Tae was translated by Chun Kyung-ja. The poems were published in the UNESCO Magazine 'Courrier'.

제2부

콩알 하나

여자의 사랑은 총알보다도 더 멀리 날아간다

불이냐 꽃이냐

너

밭 女子

이 세상에서 사라지는 것은 하나도 없다

A Single Beans

Who dropped it?

I wonder If it did'nt fall
From a hole-ridden bundle
Borne by a grandma,
All wrinkles,
Just in from the country,
On her way
To see her youngest daughter.

One green bean
trod upon, rolling
On the asphalt of the plaza
Before the depot.
That enormous life I gathered up,
Left the city behind, then

Beyond the river
Along a field's furrowed row
Planted it deep down, deep.
From all sides at that moment
Twilight was eyeing me.

콩알 하나

누가 흘렸을까

막내딸을 찾아가는
다 쭈그러진 시골 할머니의
구멍난 보따리에서
빠져 떨어졌을까

역전광장
아스팔트 위에
밟히며 뒹구는
파아란 콩알 하나

나는 그 엄청난 생명을 집어 들어
도회지 밖으로 나가

강 건너 밭이랑에
깊숙이 깊숙이 심어주었다
그때 사방팔방에서
저녁노을이 나를 바라보고 있었다.

Woman's Love Outruns a Bullet

A woman is not frail, but

Far stronger than those

Imbeciles of men.

Who were they who rushed into the

Hail of stones that day?

Who were they who rushed against the blades that day?

Who rushed into the flames, into the

Cloudburst of bullets that day?

Who rushed in wailing to rescue men,

Those who vanished, ah, buried in darkness that day?

There was no one. Though no one was there

From a distance a red moon was rising over the hill

And the women rushed forth to embrace life.

(A woman's milk is stronger than a man's blood)

In torn skirts they rushed forth.

With pomegranate breasts,

To discover the flags and

With the flags to prop up human bones.

Imbeciles! Men - common and plentiful everywhere.

Behold, woman's love indeed outruns a bullet.

여자의 사랑은 총알보다도 더 멀리 날아간다

여자는 약한 것이 아니라
여자는 시시한 바보 같은
남자들보다도 더욱 강하다
그날 돌멩이 속으로 달려간 자들은 누구였나
그날 칼날 속으로 달려간 자들은 누구였나
그날 불 속으로 총탄 속으로 달려간 자들은 누구였나
그날 사람을 구하려고 울부짖으며 달려간
오, 어둠 속으로 묻혀간 자들은 누구였나

아무도 없었다 아무도 없었지만
동산 멀리 붉은 달이 떠오르고
여자들은 생명을 껴안으려고 달려갔다
(여자의 젖은 남자들의 피보다 강하다)
여자들은 깃발을 찾으려고
깃발을 찾아서 사람의 뼈를 세우려고
찢어진 치마 석류알 가슴으로 달려갔었다
세상에 흔하디 흔한 바보 같은 사내들
보라, 여자의 사랑은 총알보다도 더 멀리 날아가지 않느냐
총알보다도 더 멀리 날아가
죽일 것도 기어이 젖가슴으로 누르고
살려낼 것은 기어이 기어이 살려낸다

It runs farther than a bullet,

Without fail presses down with breasts

What needs be killed,

And without fail resurrects, without fail,

What must be saved.

Ah, women! Even midst the flames

They blossom into flowers in the end.

Those terrifying women.

Women who, in the time, would save the whole world

Without fail.

Soul stirring women, the final face of mankind!

Women united with the last dream of mankind.

오, 여자! 불 속에서도
꽃으로 피어나고야 마는 무서운 여자
이 세상 천지를 언젠가는 구해내고야 말 여자
감격의 여자, 인류의 마지막 얼굴!
인류의 마지막 꿈으로 뭉쳐진 여자!

Flames or Flowers?

The path of flames some follow,

The path of flowers some follow.

Some speak of "History" for flames,

Some speak of "History" for flowers.

Some walk the way of wails, and

Some walk the way of songs.

Dear wayfarers, one and all!

Is the true life a flame or a flower?

Is the way of flames or of flowers the true way?

Flames brighten the darkness of night, yet

Flowers brighten the darkness of day.

Flames melt a bloodied blade, even as

Flowers cleanse the blade of blood.

The path of flames some follow,

The path of flowers some follow.

Some walk the way of wails and

Some walk the way of songs.

A way of wails and songs at once some walk.

Some follow the path at once of flames and flowers.

불이냐 꽃이냐

어떤 사람은 불의 길을 가지만
어떤 사람은 꽃의 길을 간다
어떤 사람은 불을 역사라 말하지만
어떤 사람은 꽃을 역사라 말하고
어떤 사람은 아우성의 길을 가지만
어떤 사람은 노래의 길을 간다

너희여 참삶이란 불이냐 꽃이냐
사랑의 참길이란 불이냐 꽃이냐
불은 밤의 어두움을 밝히지만
꽃은 낮의 어두움을 밝힌다
불이 피묻은 칼을 녹여버릴 때
꽃은 피묻은 칼을 닦아내는 것이다

어떤 사람은 불의 길을 가지만
어떤 사람은 꽃의 길을 간다
어떤 사람은 아우성의 길을 가지만
어떤 사람은 노래의 길을 간다
어떤 사람은 아우성과 노래의 길을 한꺼번에 간다
어떤 사람은 불과 꽃의
길을 한꺼번에 한꺼번에 간다.

You

As I ate, you died.

As I wined, you died.

As I counted money, you died.

As I lied, you died.

As I slept sweetly by my wife, you died.

As I weighed myself at a bathhouse, you died.

As I wept, though, up into Heaven you went.

너

내가 밥을 먹을 때 너는 죽었다

내가 술을 마실 때 너는 죽었다

내가 돈을 셀 때 너는 죽었다

내가 거짓말을 할 때 너는 죽었다

내가 아내와 단잠을 잘 때 너는 죽었다

내가 목욕탕에서 몸무게를 잴 때 너는 죽었다

내가 눈물을 흘릴 때 그러나

너는 하늘로 올라갔다.

Field Woman

1

A woman was giving birth someone's baby Bursting out from blazing house about to bear the baby of someone, of someone, of someone, of someone, of someone, she was weeping. And then like an immense death, she was being born. Ah, the death of a woman being born together with a blood-soaked baby, the flesh life of a woman! Amidst reports of guns firing even amidst the guns firing......

2

A woman was mending the clothes of a man. She also was mending his deep shadow, hard and deep. She was mending even the breathing he left behind. She searched out the few teardrops left by him and was mending them, too. We must go on living, now we too must live, swearing thus over and over to herself, she cleaned a plowshare. She cleaned a rake, a hoe, even a whetstone, then she lifted an A-frame onto her back. Ah, at that instant her A-frame was burdened with the breaking sun, with a long road at dawn.

밭 女子

1

여자는 누군가의 아이를 낳고 있었다. 불타는 집을 뛰쳐나와 여자는 누군가의, 누군가의 아이를 낳으며 누군가의, 누군가의, 누군가의, 누군가의, 누군가의 아이를 낳으며 울고 있었다. 그리고 여자는 거대한 죽음처럼 태어나고 있었다. 그리고 여자는 다시 어떤 거대한 삶처럼 태어나고 있었다. 아, 핏덩이의 아이와 함께 태어나는 여자의 죽음, 여자의 생살의 삶! 아, 그때 밭은 여자의 몸부림을 받아먹고 싱싱해지고 있었다. 총소리 속에서, 총소리 속에서도……

2

여자는 사내의 옷을 깁고 있었다. 여자는 사내의 그림자도 깊이깊이 깁고 있었다. 여자는 사내가 남긴 숨결마저 깁고 있었다. 사내가 남긴 몇 방울의 눈물도 찾아서 깁고 있었다. 살아야겠다고, 우리들도 이제 살아야겠다고, 여자는 몇 번이고 스스로 맹세하면서 쟁기의 보습을 닦고 있었다. 쇠스랑도 닦고, 호미도 닦고, 낫과 숫돌도 닦고, 그리고 여자는 지게를 짊어지고 있었다. 아, 그때 여자의 지게 위에 꽂혀진 새벽의 태양, 새벽의 머나먼 길!

3

Birds were fling. Dew beading on the grass was trumpeting reveille, and a woman commenced plowing "Plowing is not man's work only." she murmured. Her baby boy back over in the village was fussing for his mother's milk. She rushed over, then returned to the field with the baby on her back to plow-Sweat dripped from her breasts to moisten the earth. Beneath her feet, crumbled dirt was ready to emit green shoots. Newborn leaves! All at once she detected the sound of the river running and at long last the land of green spread open before her like a tomorrow of her very own. As though to console the child on her back, she said, "Daring, just like mama can have another baby, we always can begin anew." Till the sun sank in the west, her sweat rolled down soaking deep into the earth as she plowed on.

3

새들이 날고 있었다. 풀잎 위에 앉은 이슬들이 둥그러이 나팔을 불고, 여자는 쟁기질을 하기 시작했다. '쟁기질은 사내들만이 하는 게 아니야' 여자는 그렇게 중얼거렸다. 멀리 마을에서 아이 녀석이 젖을 주라고 보챘다. 여자는 다시 마을로 뛰어가서 아이를 등에 업고 와서 쟁기질을 계속하였다. 여자의 젖무덤에서 흘러내린 땀방울이 대지를 적시고 있었다. 여자의 발바닥 밑에서 짓이겨진 흙덩이들이 푸릇푸릇 싹을 틔우려 하였다. 새싹! 여자는 갑자기 강물소리를 들었으며, 이윽고 초록의 대지는 그녀의 내일처럼 펼쳐지고 있었다. 여자는 등에 업힌 아이에게 다짐하듯 말했다. '아가, 너의 엄마가 또 아이를 낳을 수 있듯이, 우리는 항상 다시 시작하는 거야.' 서산에 해가 떨어질 때까지, 여자는 쟁기질하며 대지의 깊숙히 땀방울을 비벼 넣었다.

Nothing in This World Vanishes

Grieve not!

Despair not!

Capitulate never!

And swallow with a gulp, with a gulp,

And live on with a kick, with a kick

From time immemorial!

Not one thing vanishes

In this world

With flowing streams and birds on wing.

As dewdrops gather and roll down

On rose petals

Everything in this broad universe

Thus smoothly thus is saturated

With perfect dreams.

Disappearing or being crushed.

Being penetrated or shrivelling.

It manifests itself only to us

Merely in form differing,

이 세상에서 사라지는 것은 하나도 없다

슬퍼하지 말라
절망하지 말라
좌절하지 말라
그리고 꿀꺽꿀꺽 먹어라
그리고 파닥파닥 살아라

이 세상에서
사라지는 것은 하나도 없다
강물이 흐르고 새가 날으던
아득한 옛날부터

장미꽃에
물방울이 맺혀 구르듯
이 세상 천지 모든 것들은
그렇게 둥그러이 그렇게
완벽한 꿈으로 젖어 있나니

사라진다는 것 부서진다는 것
구멍이 뚫리거나 쭈그러진다는 것
그것은 단지 우리에게서
다른 모양으로 보일 뿐

Like a fish in the deep.

Without losing the least bit of fin,

Survives roaming far corner of the world.

Now and again firing an arc of blue sparks.

Grieve not today!

Despair not today!

Capitulate not today!

He who grieves his heart out

Even as the horizon unfolds before his eyes,

Shall meet death by lighting.

He who despairs, who capitulates.

Even as he gazes up at the sky and down at the earth

Shall become a demon a swine.

Ah, ah, this world

Replete with mountain peaks and

Babies suckling at mothers' breasts.

Is full of fathers sowing

And spring rains and God.

그것은 깊은 바다 속의 물고기처럼
지느러미 하나라도 잃지 않고
때로는 파아란 불꽃을 퉁긴다

오늘 슬퍼하지 말라
오늘 절망하지 말라
오늘 좌절하지 말라
펼쳐진 하늘을 바라보면서
주룩주룩 슬퍼하는 자는
벼락을 맞아 죽으리라

하늘과 땅을 보면서도
절망하는, 좌절하는 자는
악마와 돼지가 돼버리리라
오, 이 세상은
아이에게 젖을 빨리는
어머니와 산봉우리로 가득하고
밭고랑에 씨앗을 놓는

Ah, ah, beneath the skies

Every corner is coated with blossoms

Of humanity's humanness!

Tears and breasts of mankind!

And two warm hands of man!

아버지와 봄비와 하느님으로 가득하다

오오, 이 세상은
아이에게 젖을 빨리는
어머니와 산봉우리로 가득하고
밭고랑에 씨앗을 놓는
아버지와 봄비와 하느님으로 가득하다

오오, 하늘 아래
빈틈없이 꽃피어 있는
사람의 사람다움!
사람의 눈물과 앞가슴!
그리고 사람의 따스운 두 손!

Part 3

Climbing Over Jirisan Mountain

Thrashing the Sesame

Persimmon Flowers

One Bean

Sword and Soil

Fire or Flower?

A Song Dedicated to Gwangju

* Dr. Chae-Pyong Song(1960~2013) was born in 1960 in Yosu, South Korea. He received his M.A. and Ph.D. in English from Texas A&M University. Since 2001, he has taught a variety of courses such as Literary Theory, World Literature in Marygrove College. He translated many of Korean poems. His website: Korean Poetry in Translation(http://yu.ac.kr/~yno1/html/main/poet.html).

제3부

지리산을 넘으며

참깨를 털면서

감꽃

콩알 하나

칼과 흙

불이냐 꽃이냐

광주에 바치는 노래

---

* 송재평 박사는 1960년 한국 여수에서 태어나 1989년 미국으로 건너갔다. 텍사스 A&M 대학에서 영문학을 전공하여 석사와 박사 학위를 받았으며 2001년 메리그로브 대학의 교수로 취임하여 문학이론, 세계문학을 가르쳤다. 특히 광주항쟁과 관련된 시편들을 열성적으로 번역하여 소개했다.

Climbing Over Jirisan Mountain

I need to talk to the clouds.

I need to talk to the wind.

I need to talk to the stepping stones by the stream.

I need to talk to the trees.

I need to talk to the cigarette butts.

Even though my words may, absurdly,

become clouds or wind,

or shake as trees at the end of December,

or fly away as sleepless birds,

or even if they become cigarette butts

that one throws away without any thought,

I need to name my words,

like the water in a kettle that overflows when it boils,

I need to scatter all of my words

over every corner of the world.

In fact, my words are their words;

my songs are their songs.

* Jirisan Mountain is located in the southern region of South Korea.

지리산을 넘으며

나는 구름에게 말해야 한다

나는 바람에게 말해야 한다

나는 시냇가 디딤돌에게 말해야 한다

나는 나무에게 말해야 한다

나는 담배꽁초에게 말해야 한다

내가 한 말이 어처구니 없이

구름이 되거나 바람이 되거나

저무는 12월 나무로 흔들리거나

혹은 불면의 새로 날아가버릴망정

무심코 던져버리는 담배꽁초가 될망정

나는 나의 말에게 이름을 붙여주어야 한다

주전자에 물이 끓으면 넘치듯이

그렇게 그렇게 나의 모오든 말을

세상 곳곳에 뿌려주어야 한다

사실은 그들의 말인 나의 말을

사실은 그들의 노래인 나의 노래를.

Thrashing the Sesame

At the corner of a farm where the mountain shadow descends,

I thrash the sesame with Grandmother.

In my eyes, Grandmother strikes the stick slowly.

But I, the young one, want to go home before dark,

and strike with all my strength.

I find rare pleasure in thrashing the sesame–

difficult to find in worldly affairs.

Since I have lived in the city for almost ten years,

it is an exhilarating thing

to watch, even with one stroke,

innumerable, white grains rushing out.

I thrash bundle after bundle, whistling.

When I am lost in thrashing,

thinking that there might be many things

that would rush out like sesame

if you gleefully strike anywhere,

Grandmother pitifully chastises me:

"Honey, don't thrash at the necks."

참깨를 털면서

산그늘 내린 밭 귀퉁이에서 할머니와 참깨를 턴다.
보아하니 할머니는 슬슬 막대기질을 하지만
어두워지기 전에 집으로 돌아가고 싶은 젊은 나는
한번을 내리치는 데도 힘을 더한다.
세상사에는 흔히 맛보기가 어려운 쾌감이
참깨를 털어대는 일엔 희한하게 있는 것 같다.
한번을 내리쳐도 셀 수 없이
솨아솨아 쏟아지는 무수한 흰 알맹이들
도시에서 십 년을 가차이 살아본 나로선
기가막히게 신나는 일인지라
휘파람을 불어가며 몇 다발이고 연이어 털어댄다.
사람도 아무 곳에나 한 번만 기분좋게 내리치면
참깨처럼 솨아솨아 쏟아지는 것들이
얼마든지 있을 거라고 생각하며 정신없이 털다가
"아가, 모가지까지 털어져선 안 되느니라"
할머니의 가엾어하는 꾸중을 듣기도 했다.

Persimmon Flowers

When I was young, I counted the falling persimmon flowers.

During the war, I counted the heads of the soldiers.

Now I count money, with spit on my thumb,

and wonder what I will count in the distant future.

감꽃

어릴 적엔 떨어지는 감꽃을 셌지
전쟁통엔 죽은 병사들의 머리를 세고
지금은 엄지에 침 발라 돈을 세지
그런데 먼 훗날엔 무엇을 셀까 몰라.

One Bean

Who spilled it?

Did it come out of

the parcel with a hole

the wrinkled country-side grandmother

was carrying on the way to see her youngest daughter?

One green bean

rolled around, trampled

on the asphalt

of the station plaza.

I picked up the tremulous life,

went outside the city,

and planted it deep, deep

into the farm furrow across the river.

Then, from every direction,

the evening glow was watching me.

콩알 하나

누가 흘렸을까

막내딸 찾아가는
다 쭈그러진 시골 할머니의
구멍 난 보따리에서
빠져 나왔을까

역전 광장
아스팔트 위에
밟히며 뒹구는
파아란 콩알 하나

나는 그 엄청난 생명을 집어 들어
도회지 밖으로 나가

강 건너 밭이랑에
깊숙이 깊숙이 심어 주었다
그때 사방팔방에서
저녁노을이 나를 바라보고 있었다.

Sword and Soil

If sword and soil

fought,

which would win?

The sword

that pierced the soil

will rust soon,

held by the soil.

칼과 흙

칼과
흙이 싸우면
어느 쪽이 이길까

흙을
찌른 칼은
어느새
흙에 붙들려
녹슬어버렸다.

Fire or Flower?

Some follow a road of fire,

others follow a road of flowers.

Some say fire is history,

others say flowers are history.

Some follow a road of cries,

others follow a road of song.

For you, what is the true life, fire or flower?

What is a true way of love, fire or flower?

Fire lights the darkness of night,

but flowers light the darkness of day.

Fire melts the blood-stained sword,

but flowers clean the blood-stained sword.

Some follow the road of fire,

others follow the road of flowers.

Some follow the road of cries,

others follow the road of song.

Some follow both roads of cries and song,

while others follow both roads of fire and flowers.

불이냐 꽃이냐

어떤 사람은 불의 길을 가지만
어떤 사람은 꽃의 길을 간다
어떤 사람은 불을 역사라 말하지만
어떤 사람은 꽃을 역사라 말하고
어떤 사람은 아우성의 길을 가지만
어떤 사람은 노래의 길을 간다

너희여 참삶이란 불이냐 꽃이냐
사랑의 참길이란 불이냐 꽃이냐
불은 밤의 어두움을 밝히지만
꽃은 낮의 어두움을 밝힌다
불이 피 묻은 칼을 녹여버릴 때
꽃은 피 묻은 칼을 닦아내는 것이다

어떤 사람은 불의 길을 가지만
어떤 사람은 꽃의 길을 간다
어떤 사람은 아우성의 길을 가지만
어떤 사람은 노래의 길을 간다
어떤 사람은 아우성과 노래의 길을 한꺼번에 간다
어떤 사람은 불과 꽃의
길을 한꺼번에 한꺼번에 간다

A Song Dedicated to Gwangju

In May, that year,

even the moon was bright in Gwangju, the City of Light

when the vampires rushed in like a gang

in chartered Honam-line trains and helicopters

to turn the whole city into a ruin.

But in Gwangju,

even the moon was bright and full

when at every door, on every street

invaders like automatons

were running around, hungry for blood.

In May, that year

Gwangju was a vast sea,

a sea where seagulls were flying,

sails were rising,

waves were rolling

where islands were wailing like people.

In May, that year

Gwangju was a solitary cross

광주에 바치는 노래

그해 5월
광주는 달도 밝았다
호남선 특별열차로
헬리콥터로 떼몰려온 흡혈귀들이
온 시가지를 쑥밭으로 만들 때

광주는 그러나
달도 둥그러이 밝았다
집집마다 거리마다
침략자와 같은 몽유병자들이
피에 굶주려 날뛸 때

그해 5월
광주는 끝없는 바다였다
갈매기가 날으고
돛이 오르고
파도가 나는 바다였다
섬, 섬들도 사람들로 울부짖는

그해 5월
광주는 고독한 십자가였다

where slaughterers were laughing

till they became bright red while they were roasting a yellow dog,

where they took away priests and monks

and beat them up till their testicles burst.

In May, that year

Gwangju was a broken cross.

It was the Buddha's naked body thrown away.

But in May, that year

Gwangju, the phoenix,

rose up again many times!

Ah, in May, that year

in Gwangju even the moon was bright.

People's hearts ran like a river of water–

even the roadside trees put their arms around them,

all the people dancing in a circle, united in this new world.

Even when the devils armed with guns and bayonets

were poking everywhere as if crazy

and the whole city rolled like a barley field,

학살자들이 황구(黃狗)를 그슬리며
시뻘겋게 웃을 때
신부와 스님들도 잡아가서
불알이 깨져라고 두들겼을 때

그해 5월
광주는 부러진 십자가였다
발가벗겨 내팽개쳐진 부처의 알몸이었다
그러나 그해 5월
광주는 또 다시 몇 번이고
치솟아오르는 불사조!

아아, 그해 5월
광주는 달도 밝았다
사람들의 마음이 강물처럼 흐르고
길가의 가로수도 어깨동무 해주고
사람 세상 통일 세상 강강술래였다

총칼뿐인 악마들이
사방팔방 미친 듯이 들쑤셔도
온 시가지가 보리밭으로 출렁이고

people cared for each other,

waved the flags of flesh and bone

along the road this land should follow.

Ah, in Gwangju, in May, that year

they knew the pleasure of living together–

joy was flapping like a sky, like a sky

where they rose up together again

even as they collapsed, dying.

사람들은 서로를 아껴주고
이 땅의 갈 길을 향하여
살과 뼈의 깃발을 흔들었다
아아, 그해 5월 광주는
함께 사는 즐거움이 있었다
함께 쓰러져 죽으면서도
함께 일어나 살고야 마는
하늘같은 하늘같은 펄럭임이 있었다

Part 4

* Kevin Ilsub Lim studied Information Management and Technology at Syracuse University in New York. He is now engaged in IT working. He translated 10 poems.

제4부

길

쌍둥이 할아버지의 노래

체옹 에크

정월단심

청천강

서산대사

향기

별

달

묘지에 대한 단상

모기소리로

＊케빈 임일섭 선생은 시라큐스 대학과 대학원에서 IT정보경영학을 공부한 후 현재 뉴욕에서 IT산업에 종사하고 있으며 이상 10편의 시를 영어로 옮겼다.

The path

Where should we go

To find our way

Fluttering directionless

Where is our way exactly

Sometimes lost in the way of people

Sometimes finding the path through people

The body that each of us carry is the path

Recognizing that truth

Surprises us to the core pleasantly

Oh, yeah, That's right......That's Right!

That at the end of furrows outskirts of the city

Tears over the sparkling eyes

The person seeding and sowing the earth through the body

    of another was the path!

길

어디로
가야 길이 보일까
우리가 가야 하는

길이
어디에서 출렁이고 있을까

더러는 사람 속에서 길을 잃고
더러는 사람 속에서 길을 찾다가
사람들이 저마다 달고 다니는 몸이
이윽고 길임을 알고 깜짝깜짝 놀라게 되는 기쁨이여

오 그렇구나 그렇구나
도시 변두리 밭고랑 그 끝에서
눈물 맺혀 반짝이는 눈동자여

흙과 서로의 몸속에 씨앗을 뿌리는 사람이 바로 길이었다.

Song of the Twins Grandfather

Piggy back on Grandfather's back,

The other one cries wanting to get a Piggyback ride too

Yea sure, Why not?

Give them both a piggy back together

They are both happy smiling in unison

I hope the North and South would be like this.

쌍둥이 할아버지의 노래

한 놈을 업어주니 또 한 놈이
자기도 업어주라고 운다
그래, 에라 모르겠다!
두 놈을 같이 업어주니
두 놈이 같이 기분 좋아라 웃는다
남과 북도 그랬으면 좋겠다.

Cheoung Ek*

Wild weeds exuberant

In a puddle

Water lilies floating about

For every soul is there a keeper**?

Upon the Shakya Tree leaves

There are starlights and floral fragrance

Which bestows upon them temporarily, There is a keeper?

September of 1975

15 kilometers south to PhnomPenh

Hundreds of babies buried

All at once in this Cheoung Ek

Ah

In this vast plain as an utter stranger

I fall into despair at the fact that I am a human being

As I kneel in front of these young death

Over Korea's Moonkyung Doldanggol

체옹 에크*

잡풀 무성한
물웅덩이에
수련 몇 송이 떠 있네

모든 영혼에는 파수꾼이 있다**?

석가나무 나뭇잎에
잠깐 내려앉기도 하는
별빛이라든가 꽃향기에 파수꾼이 있다?

1975년 9월이던가
프놈펜에서 남쪽으로 15km 지점
1백여 명의 젖냄새 아가들을 트럭에
싣고 와 한꺼번에 파묻어버린 체옹 에크!

아
이 생면부지의 벌판에 와서
나는 내가 인간이다는 사실에 절망한다
어린 죽음들 앞에 무릎 꿇어 엎드릴 때

— 코리아의 문경 새재 너머 돌당골에서

Round and round over Baksangol

Upon Hallasan's Northern Village Seashore Neobeunsungyi's
    Stonefield

Two, Three years old Babies triggered happy

Those poor young children

Far away here Cheoung Ek in this foreign country

Ah Yah Uh Yuh Oh Yoh Ooh Yoo cried in unison in Korean vowels.

---

* Cheoung Ek: Otherwise known as the "Killing Field" located close to the capital Phnom
  Pehn, Where countless people were killed in genocide.

** A Verse from the Qur'an, Chapter: "Visitors to the Room"

거창 신원 감악산 돌고 돌아 박산골에서

한라산 북촌마을 바닷가 너븐숭이 돌밭에서

두 살, 세 살 나이에 총알세례 받은 아가들!

그 어린 것들이

여기 먼 나라 체옹 에크

흙빛뿐인 물웅덩이에까지 와서

아야어여오요우유 한국어 母音으로 함께 울고 있었다.

* 체옹 에크 Cheoung Ek: 캄보디아 수도 프놈펜 근교에 위치한, 일명 킬링필드. 제노사이드 현
 장 중 하나로 가장 많은 사람이 학살당한 곳.

**이슬람 경전 『코란』의 '밤의 방문자' 장에 나오는 경구.

New Year's Single Heartedness

Went to the field on accumulated snow

And stared at the heavens and earth

Coldest three months of winter blade edged in at the tip of garlic

To not lose its spiciness

Stands more green in the snow.

정월단심(正月丹心)

눈 쌓인 밭에 가서

천지(天地)를 우러렀더니

삼동(三冬) 칼끝 입에 문 마늘촉

매운맛 잃지 않으렴인지

눈 속에 더 푸르러라.

Chungchun River

How shining she is!

Even every single pebble

She will not abandon

She will not miss

She washes away

She flows, oh, Chungchun River!

* Chungchun River: The North Korean river flowing border between Pyeonganbuk-
  do(Province) and Pyeongannam-do, previously named "Salsu" in Ancient Imperial Koguryo.

청천강

눈부셔라
조약돌 하나라도
버리지 않고
빠뜨리지 않고
씻어내리는
흘러가는 아, 청천강!

※ 청천강의 옛 이름은 '살수(薩水)'로 묘향산에서 발원하여 서해로 흘러간다.

Zen Master Seo Sahn

In my Children days

Zen Master Seo Sahn whom I met at the front yard of Haenam

    Daeheung Temple's PyoChoongSa

Did not pass away and was living in Bohyun Temple's SuChoongSa

    in the MyoHyang Mountains

Mt. Sumeru in mustard seeds dropped by the Lord Buddha

Walked in with the sounds of wind

Smiling like a big cow having survived at the 6 . 25 bombings

Up on unification I will return and rest in the mustard seed of

    Mt. MyoHyang

Grinned slightly and really

He was the man who at will moved the Mt. Sumeru

서산대사(西山大師)

어린 시절 해남 대흥사 표충사(表忠祠) 앞마당서 뵈었던 서산대사
님이

지금껏 돌아가시지 않고 묘향산 보현사 수충사(酬忠祠)에 살고 계
셨다

부처님께옵서 떨어뜨린 겨자씨 속에서 수미산 바람소리로 걸어나
오더니

6·25전쟁 때 폭탄세례를 받고도 살아남았다고 큰 소(牛)처럼 웃
으신다

통일되면 묘향산 겨자씨 속에 다시 들어가 쉬겠노라 빙긋 웃으시
었는데

정말이지, 님은 겨자씨 속에 수미산(須彌山)을 넣다 뺐다 하는 분이
었다.

Fragrance

Fragrance of an Orchid —

Couldn't be held in a pot

Not even the 700 years old Celadon pot

Nor the 500 years old Porcelain pot could fill it up.

Only the flesh and body of people

Which dissolves away like the melted candle

Could only withhold such subtle scent

Only tenacious lives filled with tears and laughter

Like a vase could withhold the fragrance

Ah, Even God, fearing it might crack

Does not lay a finger on the warm body.

향기

난(蘭)의 향기—
그릇으로는 담을 수 없다

7백년 청자 그릇, 5백년을 훌쩍
뛰어넘은 백자 그릇으로도 담을 수 없다
죽으면 촛농처럼 녹아버리는 사람들의
몸뚱이만이 그 향기 은은하게 담을 수 있다

살아서 울고 웃는 사람들의 질기고 질긴 목숨만이
꽃 항아리인 양 그 향기를 담아 넣을 수 있으렷다

아흐, 금이 갈까 봐 하느님께서도 여간해서는
손끝 하나 스치지 않는 사람의 따스한 몸뚱이!

a Star

Not only in the sky

but among people

a Star shines more

brightly Unsleeping.

별

하늘에서보다
사람들 사이에서
더 반짝이기 위해
잠 못 이룬다, 별은!

The Moon

In the land of the moon

The dead people live.

That's why,

It shines ever so bright.

달

달나라에는
죽은 사람들이 살고 있습니다.
그래서,
달은 밝습니다.

Impressions on the burial

When a King passes away

He leaves a tomb

When a common person passes away

He leaves the wind

Over the mountains, across the sea,

묘지에 대한 단상

王은 죽으면

무덤을 남기지만

백성은 죽으면

바람을 남긴다

산 넘고 바다를 건너는,

With a mosquito voice

With a mosquito voice, I yell

Even though you may not hear

With a mosquito voice, perhaps smaller than the voice of the

    mosquitoes

I yell not to kill babies in Gaza Strip.

Who, which devil, bombards, steals light of such beautiful babies' eyes?

Who breaks spectrum of lives?

I yell with a mosquito voice

Even though my mother tongue, Korean Language

Doesn't soothes smashed craniums from carpet bombing even less than

    1mm

Even though the code is lifted on the negotiation table for ceasefire

between Israel and Hamas

With a voice of a smaller than mosquitoes I yell

That killing babies are killing God.

That no war can replace peace

That no peace can be produce by war

That no more killing babies in Gaza Strip

In a small, two-parted country in the East

모기소리로

나는 모기소리로 말한다
그대들이 들을 수 없을지라도
나는 모기소리로 어쩌면 모기소리보다도
더 작은 소리이지만 Gaza지구의 아가들을
죽이지 말자고 소리친다 임산부의 뱃속까지
뒤흔들어대는 융단폭격으로 누가, 악마들이
저토록 아름다운 아가들의 눈동자에서 빛을
빼앗아가는가 생명의 스펙트럼을 박살내는가

나는 모기소리로 말한다
나의 모국어인 Korean language
폭격에 으깨져버린 아가들의 두개골을
1mm도 어루만지지 못할지라도 나의 분노가
이스라엘과 하마스의 교전중지를 촉구하는
협상테이블에서 갑자기 코드가 풀린다 하더라도

모기소리보다도 더 작지만 나는 말한다
아가들을 죽이는 것은 神을 죽이는 일이라고
어떠한 전쟁도 평화를 대신할 수 없다고 어떠한
평화도 전쟁을 통해서는 만들어질 수 없다고
동방의 작은 나라, 두 갈래로 찢어진 땅에서

I yell, scream, flutter with a mosquito voice!

Ah, you swarm of mosquitoes who rushes to sting deeply on the

Necks of lions, wolves and leopards!

Now I am born among babies in Gaza

Now I am seeing God of dead babies, in the babies' round eyes', in

immortal Gaza

Whom you can meet neither in the Bible, nor in Qur'an nor Buddhist

scriptures nor Upanishad.

더 이상 Gaza지구의 아가들을 죽이지 말라고
소리친다, 외친다, 날개를 친다, 모기소리로!

아흐, 사자와 늑대, 표범의 목에 모가지에
달려들어 깊숙이 침을 꽂는 모기 떼, 모기 떼여!
이제 나는 Gaza의 아가들 속에서 태어날 것이다
이제 나는 아가들의 둥근 눈동자 속에서 바이블에서도
코란에서도 싯다르타의 불경에서도 우파니샤드에서도 만날 수
없는, 죽을 수 없는 Gaza에서 죽은 아가들의 신(神)을 볼 것이다.

Kim Jun Tae(1948~) was born in Haenam, Jeollanamdo, Korea. He studied German literature at Chosun University. He made his literary debut in 1969 with the publication of "Thrashing the Sesame" and other poems in The Poet. His poetry collections include Thrashing the Sesame, I Saw God, The Rice Soup and Hope, Fire or Flower?, and Sword and Soil, From May to Reunification, A Sad Song of Drunkard Dreaming of Reunification, Standing on the Horizon etc. He is known as the progressive poet of 'Gwangju, Cross of Our Nation'. This poem has been acclaimed as the first poem that addressed the Gwangju uprising in 1980. He was working as a chairperson of The May 18 Memorial Foundation and is now attending a Korean literature's lecture as a inviting professor at Chosun University in Gwangju City.
e-mail kjt487@hanmail.net

김준태金準泰   1948년 전남 해남에서 태어났다. 1969년 전남일보·전남매일 신춘문예 당선, 월간 『시인』지로 나와 시집으로 『참깨를 털면서』 『나는 하느님을 보았다』 『국밥과 희망』 『불이냐 꽃이냐』 『넋통일』 『오월에서 통일로』 『칼과 흙』 『통일을 꿈꾸는 슬픈 색주가』 『꽃이, 이제 지상과 하늘을』 『지평선에 서서』 『형제』 『밭詩』 『달팽이 뿔』 등을 펴냈다. 역서로 베트남 전쟁소설 『그들이 가지고 다닌 것들』이 있으며 세계문학 기행집 『세계문학의 거장을 만나다』, 남과 북, 해외동포 시인들의 통일시에 해설을 붙인 『백두산아 훨훨 날아라』, 옛 소련 지역 한민족 구전 가요집 『재소 고려인의 노래를 찾아서』(기획, 감수) 등을 펴냈다. 고교 교사와 언론계를 거쳐 5·18기념재단 제10대 이사장으로 봉직했으며 현재 조선대학교 문예창작과 초빙교수로 재직 중이다.
e-mail kjt487@hanmail.net

Gwangju, Cross of Our Nation
아아 광주여, 우리나라의 십자가여

1판 1쇄 인쇄 2014년 12월 15일
1판 1쇄 발행 2014년 12월 23일

지은이 김준태
펴낸이 김기옥

사업3팀 최한중 **커뮤니케이션 플래너** 박진모
경영지원 고광현, 이봉주, 김형식, 임민진

디자인 소요 이경란 **인쇄** 서정문화인쇄 **제본** 정문바인텍

펴낸곳 한스미디어(한즈미디어(주))
주소 121-839 서울시 마포구 양화로 11길 13(서교동, 강원빌딩 5층)
전화번호 02-707-0337 **팩스** 02-707-0198 **홈페이지** www.hansmedia.com
출판신고번호 제 313-2003-227호 **신고일자** 2003년 6월 25일

ISBN 978-89-5975-783-1 03810